The Curse of Brian's Brick

James Andrew Hall and Judy Brown

Collins

JUMBO JETS

First published by A&C Black (Publishers) Ltd 1995
Published by Collins in 1996
10 9 8 7 6 5 4 3

Collins is an imprint of HarperCollins Publishers Ltd,
77/85 Fulham Palace Road, London W6 8JB

Text copyright © 1995 James Andrew Hall
Illustrations copyright © 1995 Judy Brown
All rights reserved.

ISBN 000-675202-0

Printed and bound in Great Britain by
Caledonian International Book Manufacturing Ltd, Glasgow

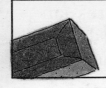

CHAPTER ONE
The Kidnapping

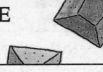

It was a Friday morning in July. Friday the thirteenth. Things were bound to go wrong.

'Oy, Brian,' said Lofty, 'lend us your brick.'

'May I borrow your brick, please?' Mrs Little corrected him.

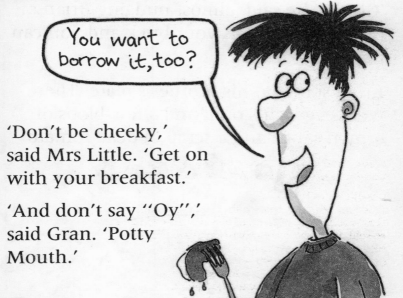

You want to borrow it, too?

'Don't be cheeky,' said Mrs Little. 'Get on with your breakfast.'

'And don't say "Oy",' said Gran. 'Potty Mouth.'

Lofty's real name was Derek. Derek Ian Mark Little, the beanpole of Spital Road. His father called him Big Dim and not just because of his initials.

His gran called him Potty Mouth. If his teacher called him anything else but Derek, it was mostly under his breath. Everyone else called him Lofty.

'Go on,' he said, almost nudging Brian off his chair. 'Lend us your brick and you can have my bacon.'

Brian stared at his brother's plate. There were egg stains on it and a few blobs of brown sauce and a scrap of dead tomato.

'You're a real pain,' said Lofty.

Brian smiled sweetly and helped himself to another bowl of Sugar Krinklies. Mr Little left the table still chewing.

Mr Little was a lorry driver. He liked to think of himself as a man of steel but kitchen foil was closer to the truth.

He delivered tinned fruit to Manchester, vacuum-cleaners to Liverpool and toilet rolls anywhere.

The toaster gave a loud bang and two slices of charred bread shot into the air. Mrs Little dived across the kitchen like a cricketer and caught them both. Brian clapped.

'Oh, yuk,' said Lofty. 'What a creep.'

'Stop getting at him,' said Mrs Little, opening a window. 'He's only four years old.'

'I'm only four years old,' said Brian, grinning like a monkey.

'You're a waste of space,' said Lofty. 'We're just letting you grow in case we need organ transplants.'

A draft from the window shifted smoke away from the toaster and blew it around Lofty.

Lofty left the kitchen, banging the door behind him. He went upstairs and looked in Brian's room. The brick was on the window-sill – but not for very long.

Five minutes later, wrapped in a scarf at the bottom of Lofty's school bag, it was waiting for a bus on the corner of Spital Road.

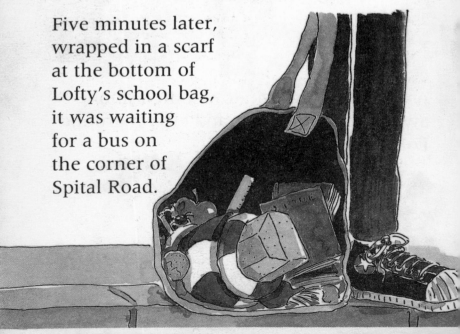

Back at home, Mrs Little pulled damp overalls from the washing machine and took them outside to hang on the line. Brian went up to his bedroom.

Left alone with the budgie, Gran sat and stared at the worst case of kitchen messiness in captivity and decided to make a hasty exit.

I'm off.

Please, oh please take me with you. They're driving me crazy!

She was in the hall putting on her coat, when Brian came tumbling downstairs.

Brick's gone!

'Poor little angel,' said Gran, rummaging in her handbag as she headed for the door. 'Have a toffee, dear. I'm off.'

Then Brian rang the police.

There was a tapping noise then, as if the voice was using a typewriter.

But there was no time to reply. Brian had seen his mother coming in from the back yard and put down the receiver.

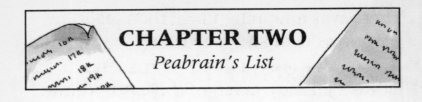

Lofty got off the bus and walked up Market Hill. His school bag was so heavy he let it drag along behind him on the pavement.

'Lofty! Yoo-hoo, cloth ears,' called Florence Jacks, running to catch up with him.

'Sandwiches,' said Lofty, knowing that Florence was daft enough to believe him.

'Wow,' she said, 'your mum must spread the butter thick.'

Florence could have won Olympic Gold Medals for Silliness.

'Do you know what day it is?' said Florence. 'It's Friday the thirteenth. Things are bound to go wrong. Our John's already fallen off his potty this morning.'

Actually, things had started to go wrong on Monday morning when Mr Perrin had pinned a list on the classroom door.

By squinting up his eyes and tilting sideways, Lofty had just been able to make out his own name and the words beside it: Friday the thirteenth.

'During the next few weeks,' said old Peabrain, leaning so far over the teacher's table that his wig shifted, 'one of you will start each day by coming our here and talking to the rest of the class. For five minutes.'

To his great surprise there was no howl of protest after this announcement. The whole class seemed spellbound.

'Talk about what?' asked Trevor Farrell.

Mr Perrin pushed his wig around until it felt more comfortable, but he could tell from Trevor's smirk that it was still cock-eyed. Whichever way he wore that wig it was always going to look like the Haircut From Hell.

'Anything that really interests you, Trevor,' he said.

Lofty decided to have toothache on Friday the thirteenth. He was quite interested in a lot of things, but not enough to talk about any of them for five minutes.

So, on Tuesday, Clive Dennis had sent them all to sleep with a five-minute talk about dinosaurs.

And on Wednesday, Winston Vicarli had startled the class with his animal impressions.

On Thursday, Florence had stopped giggling long enough to tell them about her favourite pop stars – a Scottish group called *The Poached Eggs*. She had even brought in posters and a piece of the lead singer's hair.

Jason wears a kilt and he's got smashing legs.

Now it was Friday the thirteenth and Lofty's turn. Any suggestion of toothache had been wiped out. Everyone knew that Florence had a brain the size of a pimple. If she could talk for five minutes, then so could he.

CHAPTER THREE
The Curse

'Right,' said Mr Perrin as everyone settled down after assembly, 'let's get started. Derek Little, I believe it's your turn?'

Lofty unwrapped Brian's brick and placed it on Mr Perrin's table. It looked just like any other brick – carroty colour, oblong and with a dimple in the middle of one side.

'Interesting,' said Mr Perrin, with a sinking heart. 'A house brick.'

He went to the back of the room and squeezed himself on to Lofty's chair.

Carry on, we're all ears.

'I-am-going-to-tell-you-about-this-brick,' said Lofty, talking very slowly so as to fill up his five minutes without having to say too much.

This brick belongs to our Brian. This is not just any old brick. This brick's special.

'QUIET!' roared Mr Perrin.

It was clear that this five minute talk was going to need a referee. Mr Perrin returned to the front of the class. He picked up the brick and turned it over in his hands.

Florence tried to stifle a giggle. Mr Perrin fixed Lofty with a hard stare but Lofty was gazing anxiously at the brick as if he really did expect it to be sick.

This was too much for Florence. She clapped a hand to her mouth and went bright red in the face. Giggles squeezed out between her fingers like steam.

21

'I despair of you, Derek,' said Mr Perrin. 'Haven't you got anything interesting to tell us?'

'I think our Gran's a witch,' said Lofty.

'His gran works in the greengrocers,' said Clive.

Lofty grabbed the brick from Mr Perrin and held it up.

But Lofty was enjoying himself too much to stop.

'Be warned,' Mr Perrin shouted. 'Trouble looms! Go and sit down, Derek!'

After that, Mr Perrin lost his temper. 'Sit!' he yelled. 'Now!'

He grabbed Lofty by the arm and the brick leapt from his hand.

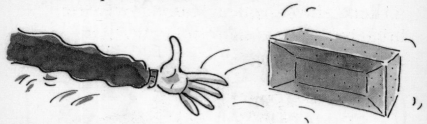

It turned a somersault . . .

. . . hit the corner of a table . . .

. . . and landed with a thud at Florence's feet.

'Great,' said Lofty. 'You've killed it!'

The whole class was silent. Lofty had gone too far this time and they knew it. All except for Florence, who was having as much fun as Lofty.

'Listen,' she squealed, leaning over the brick but not daring to touch it. 'It's saying something!'

It says Mr Perrin's hair is going to drop out and then his house will fall down and then he'll die a horrible death!

'That's enough,' said Mr Perrin, taking control of the situation. 'Florence, you can join Derek blowing up arm bands at the infants' swimming gala on Saturday.'

CHAPTER FOUR
Morning Break Blues

During morning break, Lofty hung around with Winston and Florence. Trevor dribbled a tin can up and down in front of them, using the boiler-room door as a goal.

'A magic brick,' he scoffed. 'You're out of your tree, you are. Seriously weird.'

All right, clever dick, what are you going to talk about? It's your turn on Monday.

Worms. Or sticks. Used to collect sticks. Kept them under my bed.

And you think I'm weird.

'Well, it's better than a magic brick,' scoffed Trevor. 'Only a genius could talk about sticks for five minutes.' He began prancing about heading imaginary footballs into goal.

Mr Perrin watched them from the staffroom window, clutching a mug of tea in both hands.

'Look at that lot,' he said grumpily. 'Like criminals lined up for an identity parade.'

Miss Arthur, the school secretary, glanced over his shoulder.

Whatever is the matter with Trevor Farrell? He looks as if he's rehearsing for a Grade Three ballet exam.

'I hate children,' said Mr Perrin. 'Especially boys. Especially that Derek Little.'

'What's he done now?' said Miss Arthur, helping herself to the last ginger biscuit while Mr Perrin's back was turned.

29

The bell rang for the end of break. Reluctantly, Mr Perrin made his way back to class.

Brian's brick remained on top of the stationery cupboard all day. During the afternoon, Florence scribbled a note and passed it to Lofty.

After that, Lofty stared at the brick for so long he got a crick in his neck. He thought he saw it move a little, but he could not be sure.

At home time, Mr Perrin was first through the classroom door. He almost ran down the corridor and out of the school, light-headed with relief.

What he should have been feeling was a sense of doom. Awful things were about to start happening to poor Mr Perrin.

31

CHAPTER FIVE
A Fishy Business

For the only time in living memory, Lofty was the last to leave school. When the classroom was empty, he pulled a chair over to the stationery cupboard and lifted down the brick – holding very tight in case it wriggled. He dropped it into his school bag and stuffed the scarf on top of it. If the brick spoke again, Lofty did not want to hear!

When he got outside, Florence was standing on the wall swinging her bag about in a bored sort of way.

'I didn't ask you to wait,' said Lofty as they set off down Market Hill towards Florence's house.

Florence's dad was probably the most artistic fishmonger in the country. Every morning except Sunday, he would spread out a fresh catch on wet marble and then pull a big striped blind across the pavement to keep the sun off. People came from miles around just to admire his displays.

He created fishy flags, using blue trout and silver sardines and pink salmon and yellow haddock. He could make the face of a clock with shrimp numbers and mackerel hands, or one giant fish out of lots of smaller ones.

Friday was the busiest day of Mr Jack's week and Mr Perrin was one of his regular Friday customers. He always called in on his way home from school to buy something for his tea.

But when Mr Perrin arrived outside the fish shop on this particular afternoon, he found Mr Jacks being interviewed by a reporter from *The Morning Echo*. A photographer was taking pictures of big fishy flowers on the marble slab.

'You're supposed to buy the dratted fish,' said Mr Jacks, pretending to be annoyed, 'not take snapshots of them.'

He was looking very grand in a clean striped apron and a straw hat. Florence's mother stood by his side, looking just like Florence with wrinkles.

Mr Perrin jumped up and down behind the reporter, trying to attract Mr Jacks' attention.

It was no use. After a few minutes he gave up and decided to open a tin of corned beef for his tea.

Ten minutes later, when Lofty and Florence turned the corner of Spital Road, a small crowd had gathered outside the fishmonger's. For once, nobody was admiring Mr Jacks' display. They were all staring at something rather peculiar hanging from the striped blind.

Lofty and Florence recognised the mystery object at once. It was the Haircut From Hell!

I told you, your brick's put a curse on Mr Perrin! It said he would lose his hair and now see what's happened.

Suddenly a gust of wind rippled down the blind. Mr Perrin's wig swayed gently in the breeze and then blew away. It landed on a crab, right in the middle of Mr Jacks' display. The crab looked very cosy in its fur coat.

The curse of Brian's brick, as it later came to be known, had got off to a fishy start.

 # CHAPTER SIX
Family Fury

As soon as Lofty got home, he found himself facing the fury of his whole family. Mrs Little gave him an account of the worst morning of her life (so far).

Friday the Thirteenth
Diary of Events

8.30am Toast burns. Budgie coughs a lot.

8.45am Brian finds brick missing from room and screams house down.

8.47am Brian sick on stairs – and over brand new T-shirt with a picture of The Poached Eggs.

8.50am Mrs Little rings Brian's school to say he won't be in today.

8.53am Mrs Little cleans stairs. Thinks ugly thoughts about older son.

9.30am Brian blubs. Gran arrives back from shopping and hands over tube of Smarties. Brian stops blubbing.

10.15am Brian sick again – this time in five colours. Mrs Little makes a list of ways to torture older son – thinks of seven.

'And it's all because of that brick,' Mrs Little raged, banging plates about and upsetting the budgie.

'How could you do such a horrible thing? Poor Brian's been in tears all day.'

'You ever touch Brick again,' yelled Brian, 'and you're geography.'

'It's history,' said Lofty, 'you twit.'

'Should've left you at the hospital when you were born,' said Mr Little, pointing at Lofty with his fork. All he wanted to do when he came in from work was have a shower, have a fry-up, have a sit down, have a snooze and watch the telly. Fat chance in this house.

'Why do boys have to grow up?' sighed Gran. 'They're so sweet when they're small.'

'Look at you now,' said Gran to Lofty. 'I can't believe you used to be the same size as one of your shoes.'

'It's on your head,' said Mr Little, 'if our Brian starts wetting his bed again.'

'He'll just have to sleep in the shallow end,' said Lofty, and was sent to his room without pudding.

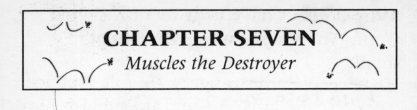

CHAPTER SEVEN
Muscles the Destroyer

After tea, Florence took the bird's nest back to Mr Perrin. Her mother had wrapped the wig in greaseproof paper like a piece of cod.

Mr Perrin's house looked haunted. It suffered from damp and stayed dismal even when the sun shone. In winter there was frost inside the windows. All he had for company was a dog called Muscles. Muscles was a wimp. He was fat and lazy and scared of rabbits. Think of a yellow cushion with fleas and you'll get the picture.

He was also very greedy.

He begged from strangers. He followed ice-cream vans. He got into rubbish bins looking for bones. He even lifted flattened chewing gum off pavements like a vacuum-cleaner.

Florence stood on the doorstep while Mr Perrin unwrapped the greaseproof.

'Am I let off helping at the swimming gala on Saturday?' asked Florence.

'No,' said Mr Perrin and Florence shuffled off pulling faces.

Before he went to bed that night, Mr Perrin laid out wig number two which he kept for special occasions like sports day and his annual holiday in Bournemouth. The wig had ginger highlights and little stickers that kept it on his head even when he swam in rough sea.

Early on Saturday morning, he was woken by the paperboy's whistling. He went downstairs and let Muscles out into the garden. Then he put the kettle on to make a cup of tea and opened the newspaper.

44

THE GRIBLEY + MIDGEFORD
MORNING ECHO

SCHOOLMASTER SCALPED!!
MYSTERY CRAB GROWS FUR!!

FIND JÖST!

The headlines were huge. They screamed at him. There was even a picture of the crab wearing the Haircut From Hell. The story took over the whole front page, except for a small report in the bottom left-hand corner:

FIND JÖST!
DUTCH TOURIST
KIDNAPPED!

Poor Mr Perrin. He forgot about Muscles. He forgot about the swimming gala. He even tried to forget about having breakfast. He just wanted the ground to open up and swallow him. He sat down at the table and stared at the paper in disbelief.

Less than a mile away, Lofty's father drove his lorry out of the supermarket depot and set off northwards with a load of toilet rolls. He was looking forward to a day of peace and quiet without any more earache about Brian's blessed brick!

As he came down the hill towards Mr Perrin's house, a yellow cushion waddled into the road with its head stuck inside an empty crisp packet.

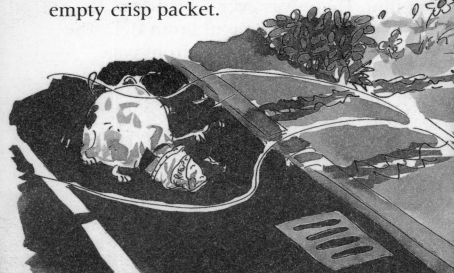

Mr Little jammed his foot on the brake pedal, swerved to avoid the dog and steered his huge lorry through a hedge, across a flower bed, over a bird-bath and straight into the side of Mr Perrin's house.

After the noise of the crash there was a terrible silence. As the dust cleared, Mr Little found himself high up in Mr Perrin's kitchen, gazing down on a bald head in a dressing gown. Mr Perrin had a mug of tea in one hand, *The Morning Echo* in the other and a gobsmacked look on his face.

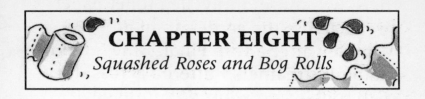
Lofty and Florence passed Mr Perrin's house on their way to school for the swimming gala. By this time, quite a crowd had gathered, with two police cars, a fire engine, an ambulance, the reporter and photographer from *The Morning Echo* and several neighbours in a dither. The lorry was still jammed inside the house like an extra room.

There was more unravelled toilet paper spread across the garden than at Wembley after a Cup Final. Blue, green and pink streamers fluttered across the brick rubble and wound themselves around people's legs.

Mr Perrin and Mr Little were sitting in deck chairs drinking tea and quite enjoying all the attention. So was Muscles.

'What's his name?' asked the reporter, making notes.

'Muscles,' said Mr Perrin.

My, that's funny. You called your dog after seafood?

She was trying to make the lorry look even bigger than it was by lying down to take pictures.

'Looks like your dad took a short cut through a brick wall,' said Florence. 'Is there a lot of madness in your family?'

At the word brick, Lofty suddenly straightened up as if someone had stuck a pin into him.

THE CURSE! It's happening. Our Brian's brick!

Don't be ridiculous! I made that up. The brick didn't really speak.

Of course it didn't, but it HEARD you!

Florence opened her mouth to say something and then closed it again when nothing came out.

'You said old Peabrain would lose his hair,' said Lofty, 'and he did. You said his house would fall down and now it has. At least, it will do when they pull out the lorry. And now he's going to die a horrible death.'

They both gazed at poor bald Mr Perrin sitting amongst his squashed roses.

Then something rather rare and wonderful happened. Giggly Florence Jacks, who gave her brain indigestion by constantly feeding it huge dollops of silliness, had an idea. Her brain gave a good burp and ping! – an idea popped up.

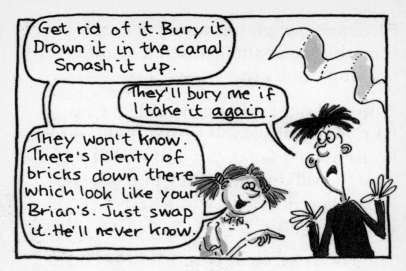

She reached through the slats of the gate and pulled out an undamaged brick.

'Right,' said Lofty, 'I'm off!' He grabbed the brick from Florence and pushed it into his school bag.

'What about the swimming gala?' said Florence.

'Get a life,' he yelled.

Florence stayed and watched as the police started clearing the garden.

'Shouldn't be hard to find him,' said the reporter. 'He'll be wearing clogs and baggy trousers and eating a bit of cheese.'

'Very comical,' said the police sergeant. 'And I suppose he'll be whistling "Tulips from Amsterdam"?'

On the way home, Lofty passed his mother going in the opposite direction. She was running. Because he was supposed to be at school, he hid in a doorway.

Mrs Little tore by without seeing him. She was still wearing an apron. Lofty guessed that someone had rung her about the crash and felt a bit guilty. He should have called out and told her not to worry.

Just in case he was spotted in Spital Road, he used the alley behind the house. It was so gloomy that an elephant could have wandered along without being seen. As he reached the back gate, he could hear Brian playing Space Invaders with Mrs Hinton next door.

Using the key his mother kept under a flower pot, Lofty let himself in by the kitchen door. The house was very quiet. Even the budgie seemed to be asleep on his perch.

Lofty yanked Mr Perrin's brick from his school bag and took it upstairs. As usual, Brick was standing on the window-sill in Brian's bedroom. Lofty picked it up with his free hand and held the two bricks together. They looked identical.

He put Mr Perrin's brick on the window-sill and then left. He let himself out of the kitchen door, replaced the key, and ran back down the alley.

CHAPTER TEN
A New Mr Perrin

By Monday, things were definitely looking up for Mr Perrin. 'The Curse of Brian's Brick' was almost hidden in the middle of *The Morning Echo*. There was a very small picture of the lorry sticking out of the house and only a few words of explanation under the headline:

Hairless boffin in accident riddle

The front page of the newspaper was filled with news about the Dutch tourist:

'What did you do with your Brian's brick?' asked Florence on the bus to school.

'Chucked it into Old Peabrain's garden,' said Lofty. 'Hope I got the right brick. The curse might still be working.'

But there was Mr Perrin safe and sound at Assembly and looking ten years younger without a wig!

'I feel as if a great weight has been lifted off my mind,' he said, 'especially as term ends on Wednesday.' He examined the list on the door.

'Trevor!' he said. 'Your turn today. Come out here and knock our socks off.'

Trevor opened his desk and lifted out a jam-jar.

'What's that?' asked Mr Perrin suspiciously.

WORMS!

CHAPTER ELEVEN
The End of Brian's Brick

This is where things get cleared up so that everyone lives happily ever after . . . fat chance! First of all, Lofty's father was given a new job behind a desk at a supermarket depot. This suited him fine because he had lost his nerve driving a big lorry. It also meant he could stay in bed later every morning.

Then Brian was five and Gran gave him a Junior Computer for his Birthday. A computer and a brick? No contest. Brick got the old heave-ho.

'I only liked it a bit,' he said, dumping it in the back alley. 'It's eyes are too close together.'

For a while, Mrs Little used it as a weight to keep the bin lid from blowing away. One day it fell into the bin by mistake and was never seen again.

A bulldozer finished what the lorry had started and knocked down the rest of Mr Perrin's damp old house. While he and Muscles were away in Bournemouth on their long summer holiday, a very nice bungalow was put together for them on the same site.

The builders used some of the undamaged bricks they found lying around in the garden. One of them was Brian's real brick!

It is now part of the bungalow chimney, but much too high up to be of any trouble.

'I'm still here,' it screams. 'I've been bricknapped!'